XTREME SC

THE WORLD'S MOST MENACING
Mummies

A&D Xtreme
BOLD HI-LO NONFICTION

An imprint of Abdo Publishing
abdobooks.com

S.L. HAMILTON

TAKE IT TO
THE XTREME!

GET READY FOR AN XTREME ADVENTURE!
THE PAGES OF THIS BOOK WILL TAKE YOU INTO THE THRILLING
WORLD OF THE MOST MENACING MUMMIES ON EARTH.
WHEN YOU HAVE FINISHED READING THIS BOOK, TAKE THE
XTREME CHALLENGE ON PAGE 45 ABOUT WHAT YOU'VE LEARNED!

ABDOBOOKS.COM

Published by Abdo Publishing, a division of ABDO, PO Box 398166, Minneapolis, Minnesota 55439. Copyright © 2022 by Abdo Consulting Group, Inc. International copyrights reserved in all countries. No part of this book may be reproduced in any form without written permission from the publisher. A&D Xtreme™ is a trademark and logo of Abdo Publishing.

Printed in the United States of America, North Mankato, MN.
032021
092021

**THIS BOOK CONTAINS
RECYCLED MATERIALS**

Editor: John Hamilton; Copy Editor: Bridget O'Brien

Graphic Design: Sue Hamilton

Cover Design: Laura Graphenteen

Cover Photo: iStock

Interior Photos & Illustrations: Alamy-pgs 23 (inset), 26, 28-29 & 32-33; Ancient Origins-pg 31 (top); AP-pgs 20, 22-23 & 27; Capcom-pg 42; Dell Comics-pg 39 (bottom); Friends of the Past-pg 30; Getty-pgs 10-11 & 24-25; Hammer Comics-pg 39 (middle); Harper & Brothers-pg 38; Harry Burton-pgs 6-7; iStock-pg 1 (mummy); NASA-pg 1 (Moon); Nevada State Museum/Denise Sins-pg 31 (bottom); Nintendo-pg 43 (bottom inset); Riot Games-pg 43; Robert Dalrymple-pgs 22-23; Scholastic-pg 39 (top); Science Source-pgs 14-15 & 16-17; Shutterstock-pgs 4-5, 8-9, 9 (top), 12-13, 18, 19, 34-35 & 44; Universal Pictures-pgs 36-37, 40 & 41; Wikimedia-pg 21

LIBRARY OF CONGRESS CONTROL NUMBER: 2020948044

PUBLISHER'S CATALOGING-IN-PUBLICATION DATA

Names: Hamilton, S.L., author.

Title: The world's most menacing mummies / by S.L. Hamilton.

Description: Minneapolis, Minnesota : Abdo Publishing, 2022 | Series: Xtreme screams | Includes online resources and index.

Identifiers: ISBN 9781532194870 (lib. bdg.) | ISBN 9781644946251 (pbk.) | ISBN 9781098215187 (ebook)

Subjects: LCSH: Mummies--Juvenile literature. | Mummies in mass media--Juvenile literature. | Mummy films--Juvenile literature. | Mummies in literature--Juvenile literature. | Monsters--Juvenile literature.

Classification: DDC 398.2454--dc23

TABLE OF
Contents

CHAPTER 1
THE WORLD'S MOST MENACING
Mummies

Mummies are bodies of the dead. Legends say they return to life to enact an ancient **curse** or punish the wrongdoers who entered and stole from their tomb. Once awakened, they have strength and supernatural powers.

XTREME FACT

An Egyptian mummy was aboard the *Titanic* when the ship sank in 1912. Some blame the mummy's curse for the ship's sinking.

CHAPTER 2

History

Mummies have been found in cultures around the world. Some were created accidentally and some were purposely mummified in religious services for the dead.

The most famous mummy ever found was Egypt's King Tutankhamun. Howard Carter discovered the secret burial chamber filled with treasure in 1922.

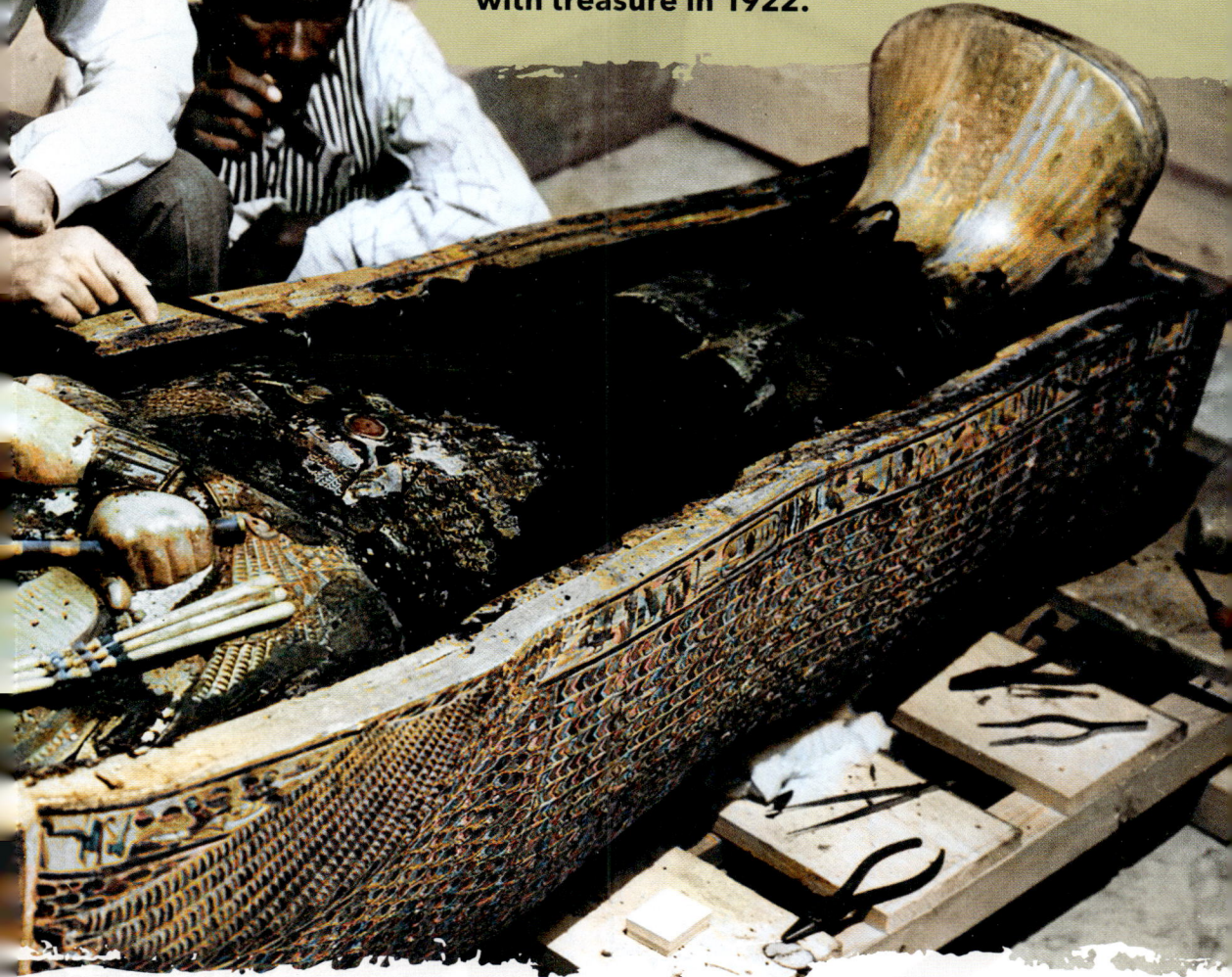

Tales of mummies coming alive and attacking or **cursing** humans have been told for centuries. These legends became popular in the Western world as **archaeologists** began discovering Egypt's mummies in the 1800s.

CHAPTER 3

Becoming a Mummy

A body becomes "mummified" when **bacteria** cannot grow and break down the dead tissue. Humans, as well as dogs, cats, monkeys, kangaroos, falcons, and other animals have been found mummified.

Mummified Cat

Mummified
Kangaroo

Natural mummification happens accidentally. A body may become mummified by being placed in extremely dry, hot, or cold temperatures where it cannot **decompose**.

A baby naturally mummified by the cold was found with seven other mummies in Greenland. It's estimated that the people died around 1475 AD.

Bacteria also cannot grow in sulfur, salt, or peat. Mummies have been found in mines containing these minerals, as well as in **peat bogs**.

Mummies may be created on purpose to **preserve** the dead. Chemicals keep **bacteria** from breaking down a body. Natron, a naturally occurring mix of salt and baking soda, was used to dry out tissue.

Bodies were then further protected with a coating of fats, waxes, or oils. This kept moisture in the air and in underground burial locations from getting to the body.

Embalmers wrapped each toe and finger and then more and more of a body. They often used 100 feet (30 m) of linen, cut into strips, to cover all of a person.

Jegou.

A dead person was wrapped in strips of linen. This fabric, often coated with a **resin**, kept moisture from decaying the body. The fabric also helped **embalmers** fill out the body to make it look more lifelike in size. **Amulets** were placed between the linen wrappings or words written on the linen, to protect the dead from mishap.

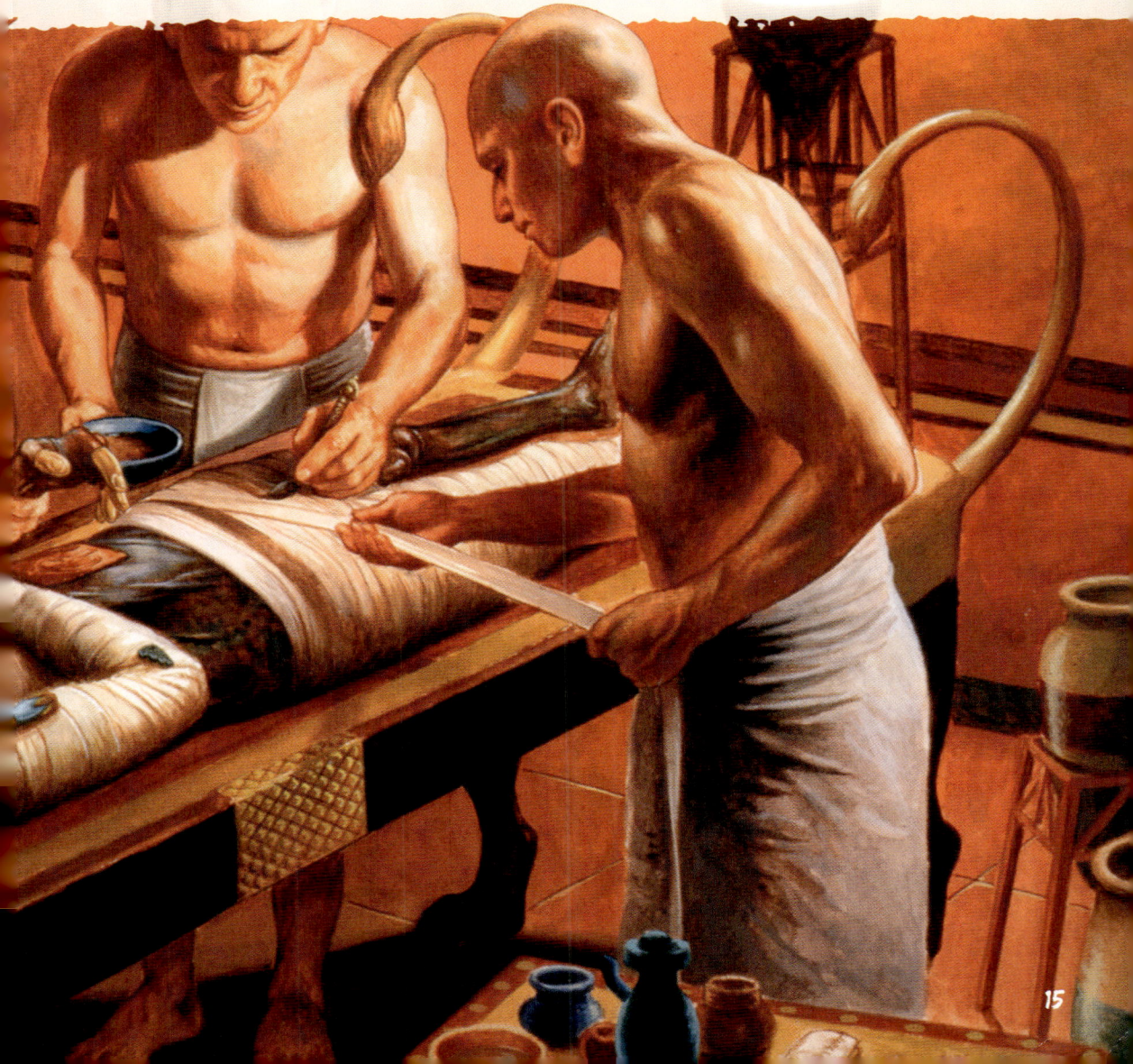

CHAPTER 4

MUMMIES
Around the World

The ancient Egyptians are the most famous mummy makers. They believed that once someone died, their soul needed a **preserved** body to live on in the hereafter.

XTREME FACT

Preserved Egyptian mummies have been found that are more than 5,000 years old.

Egyptian priests and workers perfected their **embalming** skills. Their techniques were often very secretive. It could take several months before a body was dried, wrapped, blessed, placed in a **sarcophagus**, and finally ready for burial.

Egypt's Pharaoh Ramses II's mummy is more than 3,255 years old.

In the areas of Australia, Torres Strait Islands, and Western New Guinea, bodies were smoked to create mummies. The dead were placed on a platform, a fire built, and over the course of several weeks, the smoke created mummified remains.

The smoked mummified remains of a great ancestor from the Dani tribe of Western New Guinea, Indonesia

This Dani tribe mummy is about 300 years old.

New Zealand's Maori tribes sometimes kept the mummified heads of important tribe and family members, as well as those of their enemies. The heads were called mokomokai. The uniquely tattooed heads were highly valued.

Many mokomokai heads once displayed in museums have been returned to New Zealand for proper burial.

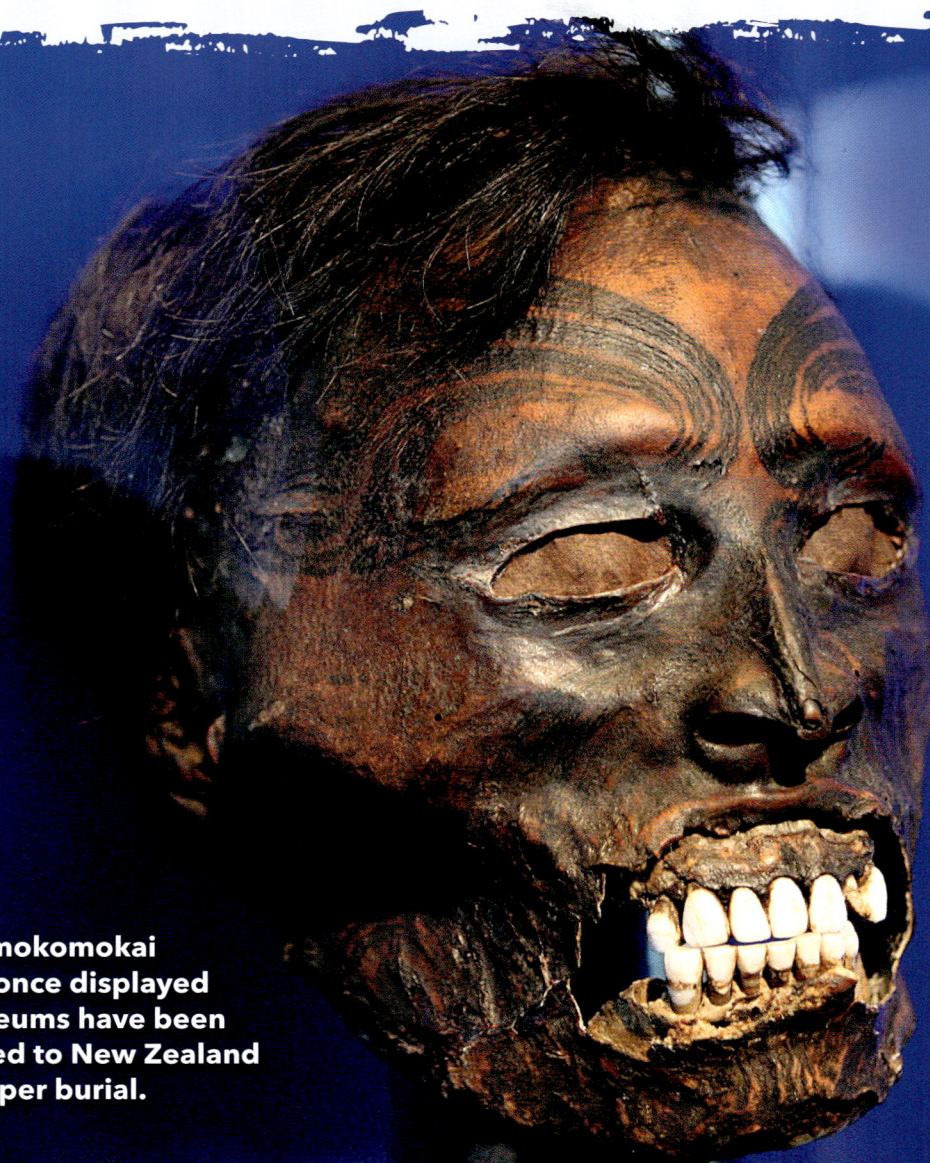

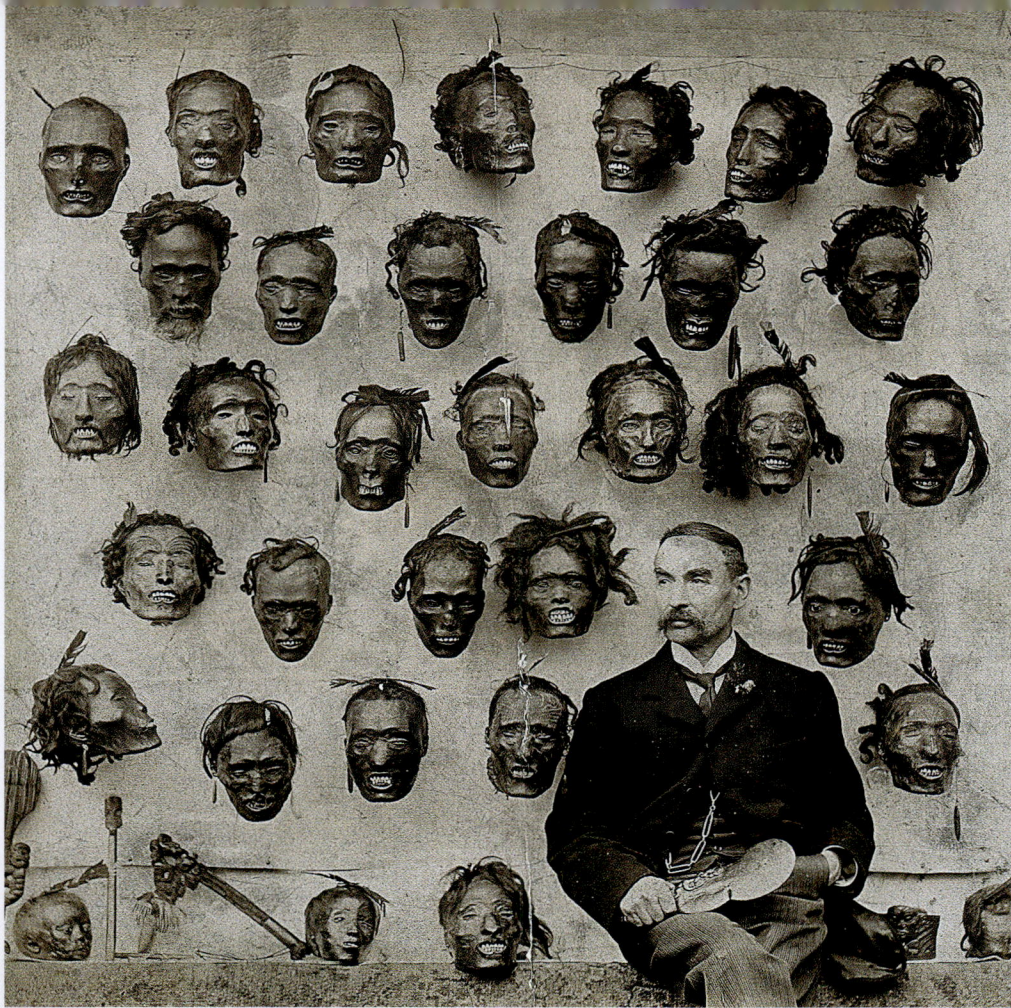

Mokomokai were eagerly bought by the British in the 1800s and early 1900s. Major-General Horatio Gordon Robley used his mokomokai for scientific study. He sold his collection to the Museum of Natural History in New York.

XTREME FACT

Mokomokai heads were once so popular that slaves were sometimes tattooed, murdered, and the heads mummified to sell to European collectors.

"The man in salt" remains in the Austrian mine in which he died.

Mummified bodies have been discovered in salt mines. The oldest salt mine in the world is in Hallstatt, Austria. In 1734, a mummified miner was found buried in salt from a cave-in 2,500 years ago. In 1993, a body and **artifacts** were found in a salt mine in Zanjan, Iran. Called Salt Man 1, he died from a tunnel collapse around 300 AD.

Salt Man 1 is at the National Museum of Iran in Tehran. Other mummies, some even older, have been found in the same mine.

Denmark's Tollund Man is a mummy discovered in a **peat bog** in 1950. He died about 350 BC. Acid and lack of oxygen in the peat bog's water kills **bacteria**. Tollund Man was **preserved** so well that the people who found him thought he had recently died and called the police.

Tollund Man died by hanging. The rope was still around his neck when he was found.

XTREME FACT

Tollund Man was so well-preserved in the peat bog, scientists could tell what he ate for his last meal.

The freezing, dry air of South America's Andes Mountains created mummies of native Inca sacrifices from more than 500 years ago. The frozen body of Mummy Juanita was found in 1995. Three child mummies were found at a gravesite near the top of the Llullaillaco volcano in 1999.

Mummy Juanita

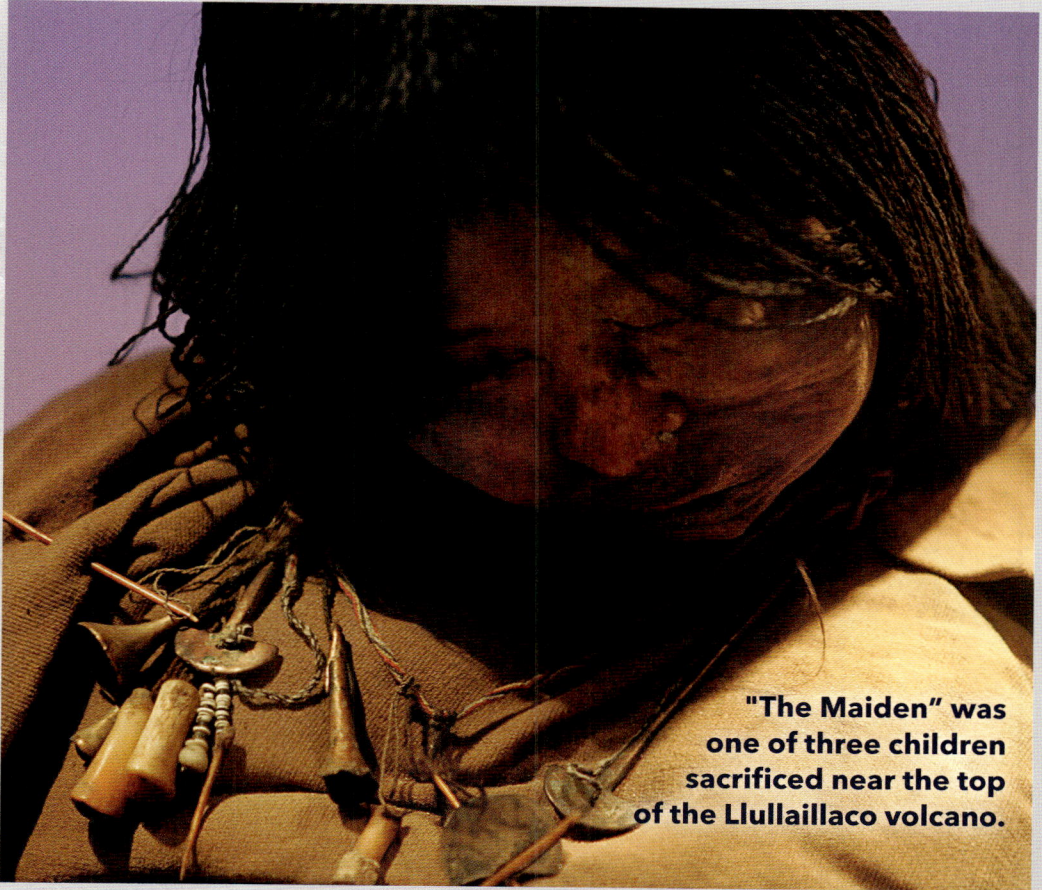

"The Maiden" was one of three children sacrificed near the top of the Llullaillaco volcano.

XTREME FACT

The Children of Llullaillaco are said to be the best preserved Inca mummies ever found. The bodies froze before they could begin to decompose. Internal organs and even blood were still inside the bodies.

From 1865–1958, the town of Guanajuato, Mexico, required a grave tax from living relatives of the cemetery's dead. If family members didn't pay, the corpses were dug up and stored in a room until the tax money was received.

The very dry conditions of the soil naturally mummified the dead. The bodies showed the gruesome way they dried. Viewing the stored bodies became popular. Eventually the room became the Museum of the Mummies.

Today, visitors see the Guanajuato mummies in glass cases at the Museum of the Mummies.

The Spirit Cave Man is the oldest mummy found in the United States. The 10,600-year-old remains were discovered in a shallow grave in a rocky shelter in Nevada. The body was wrapped in mats made of a marsh plant called tule. These protective mats and the very dry cave mummified part of the body.

Spirit Cave Man was found in 1940. His body was wrapped in a rabbit-skin blanket and he wore moccasins on his feet.

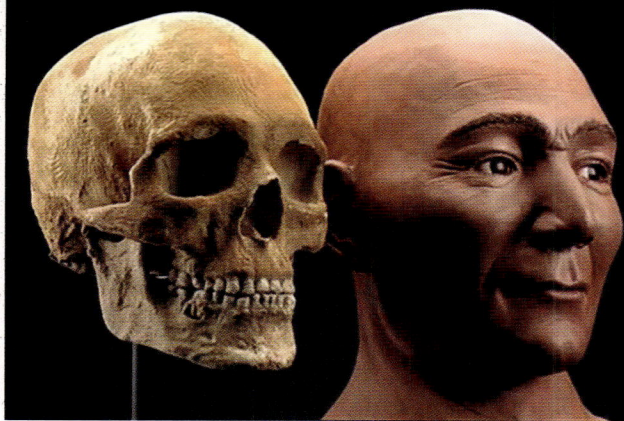

Scientists determined that Spirit Cave Man was about 40 years old when he died. He was a Native American ancestor of the Fallon Paiute-Shoshone people.

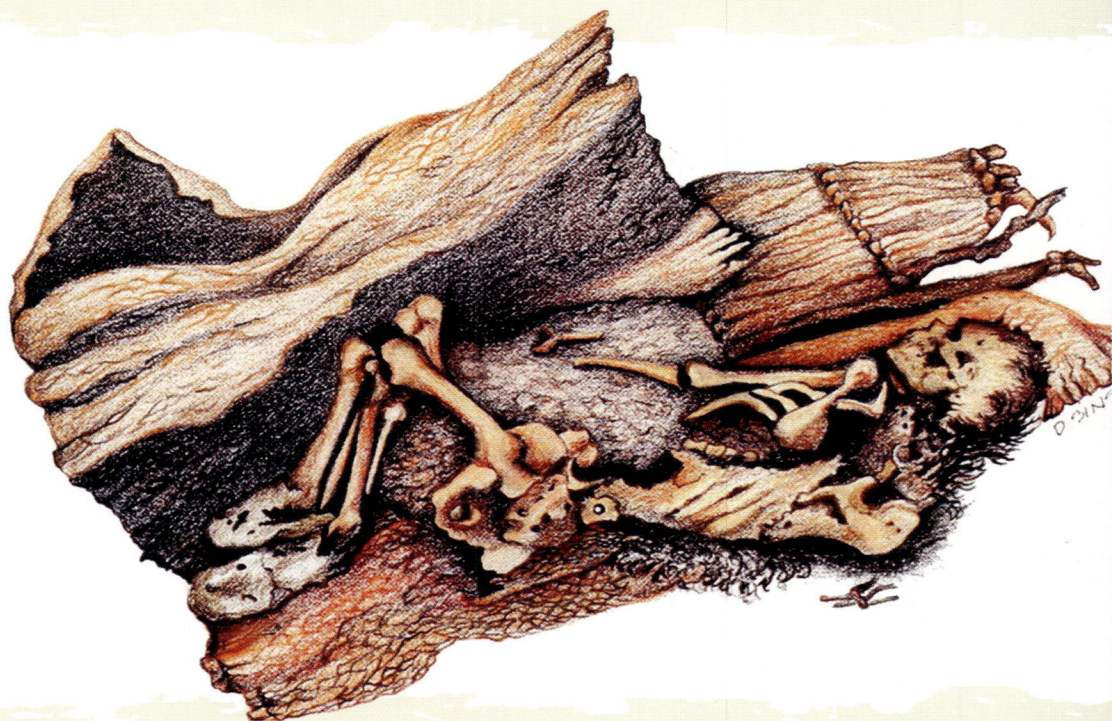

XTREME FACT

The remains of Spirit Cave Man have since been buried by the Fallon Paiute-Shoshone tribe.

Russia's Siberian Ice Maiden's frozen grave was found in 1993 in the Altai Mountains on the Ukok Plateau. She was named Princess Ukok. She was buried in fine clothing, a headdress, jewelry, and with six horses.

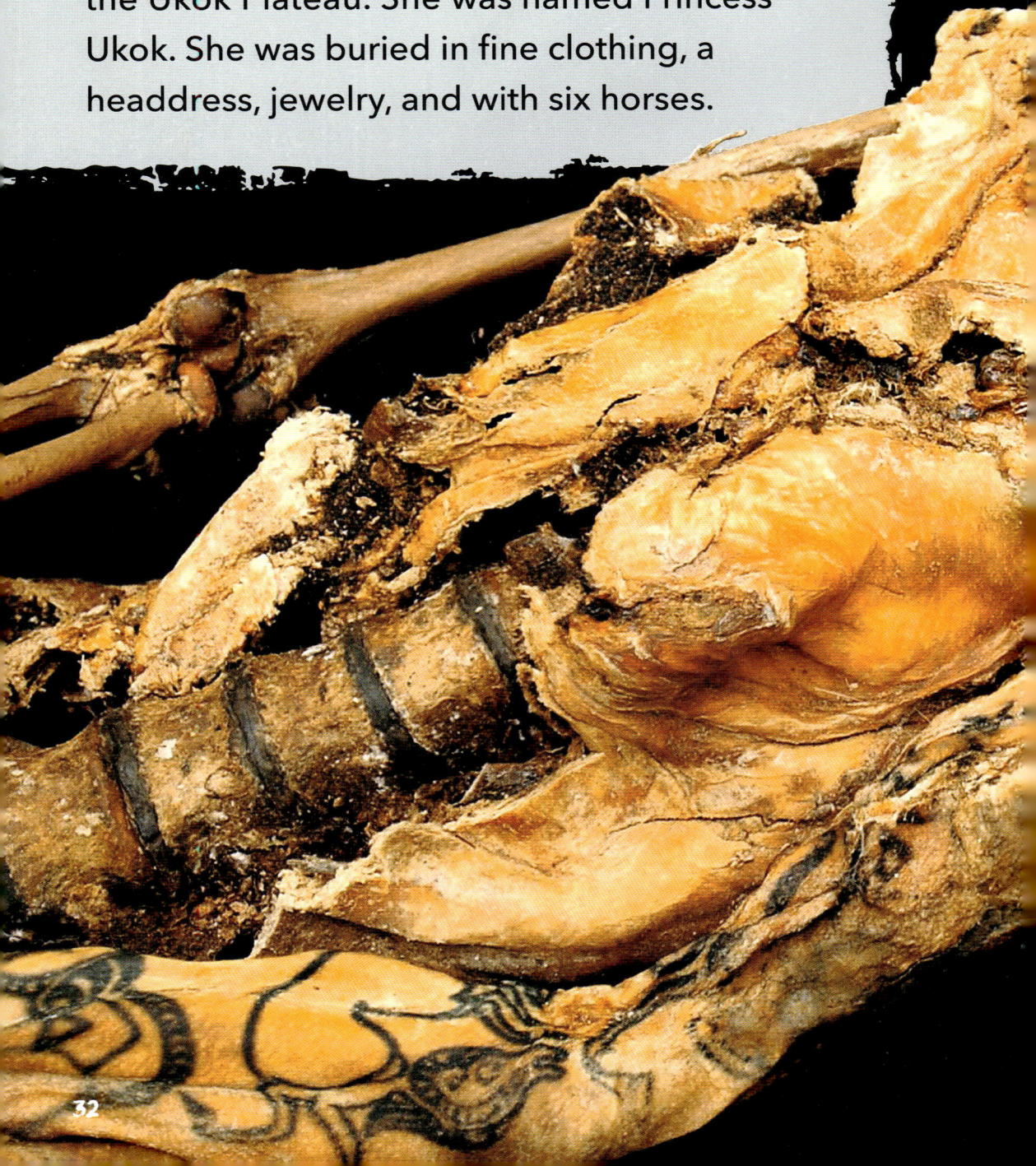

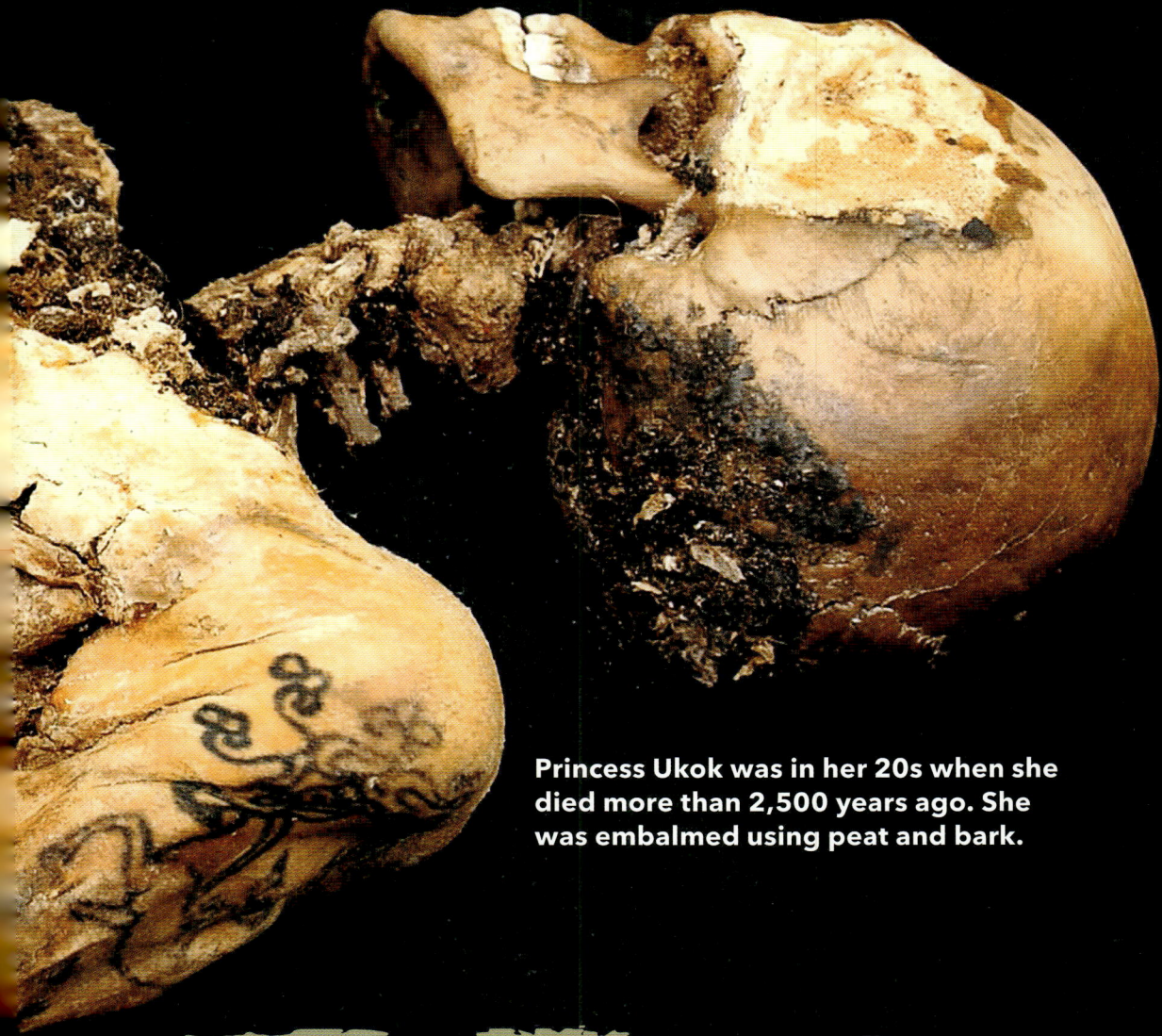

Princess Ukok was in her 20s when she died more than 2,500 years ago. She was embalmed using peat and bark.

XTREME FACT

Princess Ukok had several tattoos on her skin. The stylized deer on her shoulder became famous.

CHAPTER 5

BRINGING A
Mummy to Life

How do **fictional** mummies come to life? Usually magical words read aloud provide life to those once dead. Or if someone disturbs a mummy's slumber, the dead one awakens for revenge.

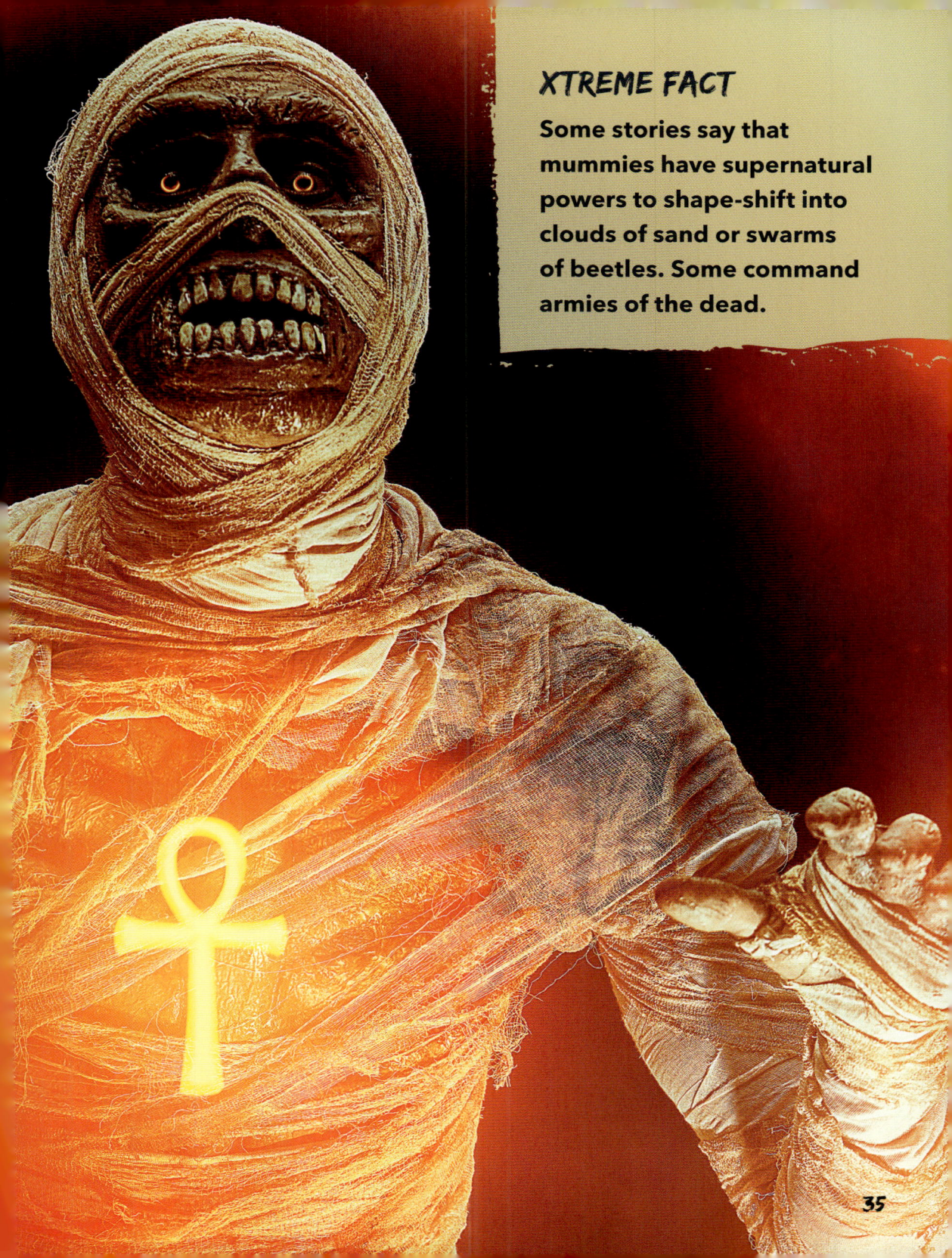

XTREME FACT

Some stories say that mummies have supernatural powers to shape-shift into clouds of sand or swarms of beetles. Some command armies of the dead.

CHAPTER 6

HOW TO KILL A
Mummy

How are mummies killed if they are already dead? Stories say that bullets, knives, and ropes have no effect. However, the dried-out mummies cannot survive fire. Also **incantations** could send them back to the hereafter.

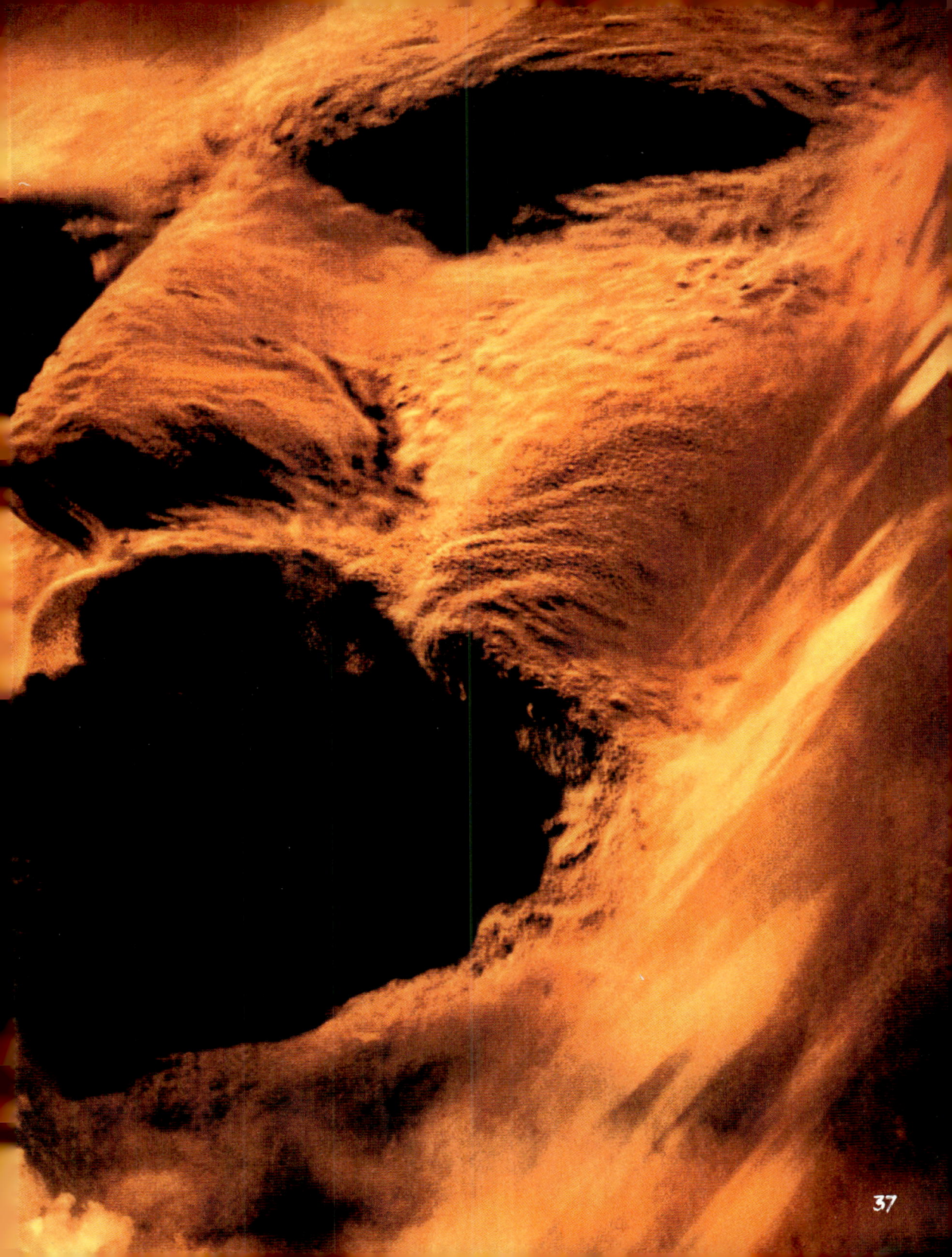

CHAPTER 7
MUMMIES
In the Media

Many books bring mummies to life. Bram Stoker wrote *The Jewel of Seven Stars* in 1903. His **fiction** story featured an **archaeologist** who wanted to revive an ancient Egyptian queen. Hundreds of terrifying mummy-themed stories followed by many authors.

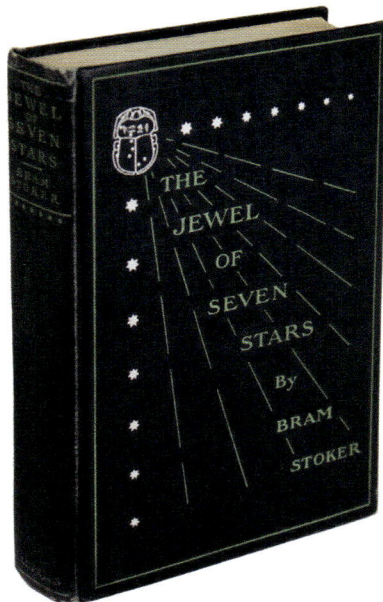

Horror author Bram Stoker, famous for his 1897 *Dracula* book, also wrote *The Jewel of Seven Stars*. It was one of the first mummy books.

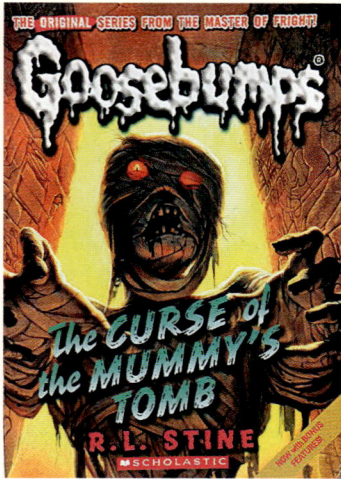

The Curse of the Mummy's Tomb cover

R.L. Stine's Goosebumps series has several mummy stories, including *The Curse of the Mummy's Tomb.*

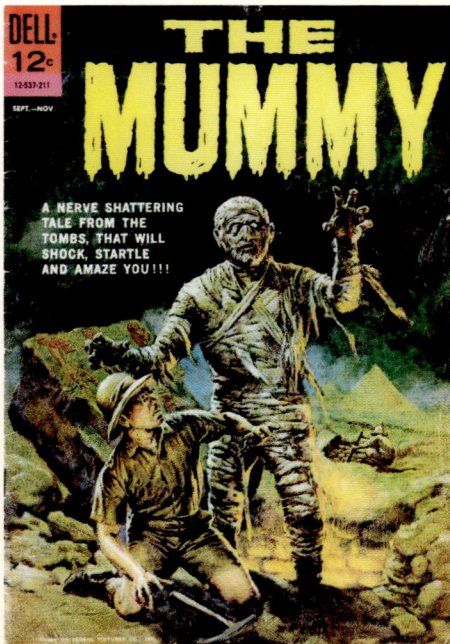

The Mummy Palimpsest cover

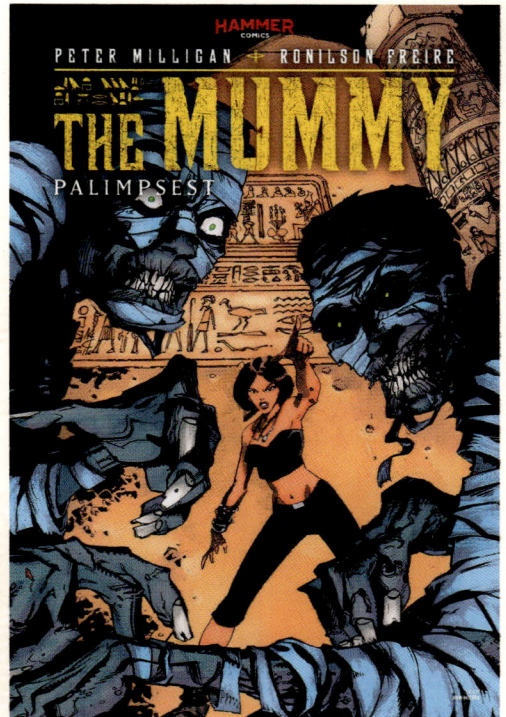

The Mummy (Dell Comics) cover

Comic books have featured mummies for decades. These include Dell Comics' *The Mummy* and Hammer Comics' *The Mummy Palimpsest.*

Universal Pictures' 1932 film *The Mummy* was the first major mummy motion picture. It starred Boris Karloff. The studio made many other mummy movies over the years, including a popular series from 1999-2008 and a 2017 film.

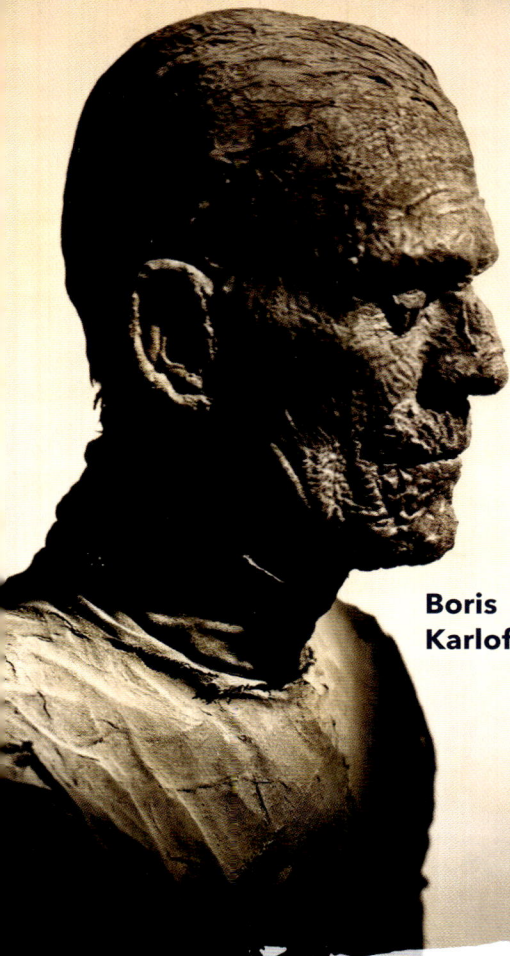

Boris Karloff

The Mummy was recreated in a popular movie series from 1999-2008 (below) and in a feature film in 2017 (right).

WELCOME TO A NEW WORLD OF GODS AND MONSTERS

THE
MUMMY

Mummies are known for power, spells, and **curses**. Mummy game characters often blend these strengths with their weaknesses, such as slow, stumbling walks and **fragile** bodies.

Capcom's _Darkstalkers_ games include the mummy Anakaris. The former pharaoh has been brought back to life with strength and unique powers.

In Riot Games' *League of Legends*, Amumu the Sad Mummy roams the world in search of a friend. But an ancient curse means his touch is death and his friendship doom.

XTREME FACT

Most game mummies are bandage-wrapped walkers, but a few, such as Pokémon's Cofagrigus, carry their sarcophagi with them.

CHAPTER 8
ARE SUPERNATURAL MUMMIES
Real?

Real mummies are found all around the world. However, the bodies are **fragile** and do not come back to life. Some people think mummy **curses** are real. Most believe it is a way to stop grave robbers from stealing from the dead.

Peru's Inca mummified their dead rulers and kept them with the tribe.

XTREME
Challenge

1) Who is the world's most famous Egyptian mummy? What year was he found?

2) Besides humans, what other living things may become mummified?

3) How can a body become mummified naturally?

4) Natron was used to dry out a dead body. What two common substances is it made of?

5) What kind of fabric was used to wrap Egyptian mummies?

6) Which country and tribe kept mummified heads of important family and tribe members, as well as those of their enemies?

7) In fiction, how do mummies come to life? How are they killed?

Glossary

amulet – A small object worn as a charm against evil.

archaeologist – A scientist who studies physical objects to learn about historic people, their activities, and practices.

artifacts – Objects from the past, often items made by humans.

bacteria – Single-celled organisms that break down tissue and often cause illness and disease in humans.

curse – A series of words or a wish for something bad to happen.

decompose – To rot or decay. Usually, the tissue of once-living things, such as humans, animals, and plants, begins to decompose as soon as they die.

embalmers – People whose work is to keep a dead body from decaying.

fiction – Stories that are made up by a writer or speaker. Not fact.

fragile – Easily broken or hurt. Something that must be handled with extreme care.

incantation – A series of special words spoken aloud that produce a magic spell.

peat bog – A kind of wetland. Lots of dead plant material, called peat, builds up in the water. This makes the water mildly acidic, which kills bacteria. Also, oxygen is used up in bogs, which slows down decay.

preserve – To keep something from rotting or decomposing. Mummified bodies have been preserved.

resin – A sticky yellow or brown substance that is often made from tree sap. It may be used as a coating over a mummy's wrappings to keep out wetness and prevent rotting.

sarcophagus – A coffin.

Online Resources

Booklinks
NONFICTION NETWORK
FREE! ONLINE NONFICTION RESOURCES

To learn more about the world's most menacing mummies, please visit **abdobooklinks.com** or scan this QR code. These links are routinely monitored and updated to provide the most current information available.

Index